MORTON PUBLIC LIBRARY DISTRICT

A13001 293558

JP LAB Blue
Labaronne, Charlotte.
Best friends

W9-AUT-292

Pour Maman et Juliette
— C. L.

Text and illustrations copyright © 2001 by Siphano Picture Books

First published in the United Kingdom in 2001 by Siphano Picture Books Ltd.

All rights reserved. Published by Orchard Books, an imprint of Scholastic Inc.
ORCHARD BOOKS and design are registered trademarks of Watts Publishing
Group, Ltd., used under license. SCHOLASTIC and associated logos
are trademarks and/or registered trademarks of Scholastic Inc.

No part of this publication may be reproduced, or stored in a retrieval system,
or transmitted in any form or by any means, electronic, mechanical, photocopying,
recording, or otherwise, without written permission of the publisher. For information
regarding permission, write to Orchard Books, Scholastic Inc., Permissions Department,
557 Broadway, New York, NY 10012.

Library of Congress Cataloging-in-Publication Data
Labaronne, Charlotte.
Best Friends / Charlotte Labaronne. — 1st ed.
p. cm.
Summary: On Louise the lion's first day of school,
Alexander the alligator wants to make friends,
but he does not know how to talk to her.

ISBN 0-439-37252-6

(1. Alligators — Fiction. 2. Lions — Fiction. 3. Friendship — Fiction.
4. First day of school — Fiction. 5. Schools — Fiction.) I. Title.
PZ7.L1115 Al 2003
(E) — dc21   2002066244

10 9 8 7 6 5 4 3 2 1   03 04 05 06 07

Printed in Singapore   46

Reinforced Binding for Library Use
First Scholastic edition, July 2003

The display type was set in Coop Black.
The text type was set in 17-point Benguiat.
Book design by Yvette Awad.

BEST
FRIENDS

Charlotte Labaronne

ORCHARD BOOKS
An Imprint of Scholastic Inc.
New York

MORTON PUBLIC LIBRARY DISTRICT
315 W. PERSHING
MORTON, ILLINOIS 61550

Alexander the alligator was sad.

He didn't have any friends.

At story-time, Alexander decided that
the drum would be a good playmate.
He walked around beating the drum.

BOOM! BOOM! BOOM!

But the drum was too loud, and it
didn't talk back.

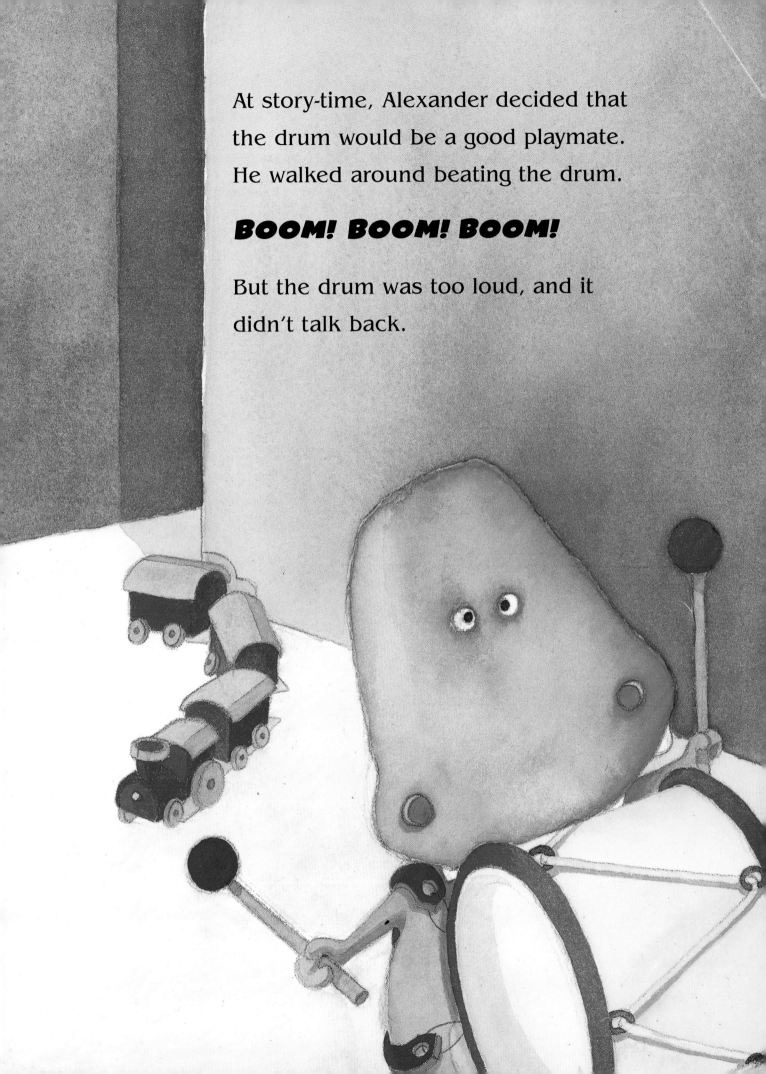

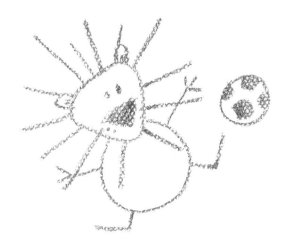

At drawing-time, Alexander heard
Katie the beaver talking about
a new kid coming to school.
She was a lion named
Louise.

"Maybe Louise will be my friend,"
thought Alexander.

The next morning, Alexander waited
for a long time at the school gate.
Louise finally appeared.

"Hi," she said. "My name is Louise."

But Alexander did not know what to say.

The other children introduced themselves
to Louise and invited her to play with them.

Alexander picked up a soccer ball,
thinking Louise might like soccer,
but she was already playing with
the other kids.

Alexander felt left out.

Alexander came up with a plan to get Louise's attention.
He squirted some orange juice on her teddy bear.

But she did nothing.

He was just about to run over her teddy bear,
but he realized that Louise wasn't even looking at him.

When he saw Louise
building a tower of blocks,
he walked past and gave it a kick.
The blocks came down with a
CRASH,
but Louise didn't do a thing.

Then he got out his tuba and blasted it in her ear.

Still, nothing.

So when she went over to paint,
Alexander found a can of red paint . . .

. . . and splashed red spots all over her paper.

THAT DID IT!

Louise opened her mouth and let out one enormous, terrifying

ROARR

Alexander jumped back.
He had never heard
anyone make a noise
like that before.

RRRR!

"Oh my!" thought Alexander.
"That was not such a good plan."

Alexander was afraid of Louise,
and so he decided to stay inside
while Louise and all the other kids
went outside to play.

After a while, Louise came inside.

"Why don't you like me?" she asked.

"I thought you didn't like me," Alexander answered.

"Come with me," said Louise.

Louise climbed on the seesaw and asked
Alexander to sit on the other side.

"I hope she doesn't ROAR at me again!"
Alexander thought.

After they seesawed for a while, they decided to ride on the tire swing. Some of the other kids came to play on it, too.

Then they played on the climbing bars.
Alexander was having a lot of fun with Louise.

Alexander saw Louise opening her mouth.
"Oh, no!" he thought. "Here it comes!"

"WILL YOU BE MY BEST FRIEND?" roared Louise.

"Yes!" said Alexander.

When story-time came, Alexander
sat next to his new friend, Louise.

Afterward, the teacher looked at
Louise and asked, "How was your
first day at school, Louise?"

"Great," she answered, "I have
a new best friend named Alexander."

Alexander smiled and thought, "And I
have a new best friend named Louise."